# Cowboys

Gorsline

A Random House PICTUREBACK®

# Cowboys

## by Marie and Douglas Gorsline

RANDOM HOUSE 🏠 NEW YORK

More than a hundred years ago, millions of longhorn cattle roamed the Texas plains. There was plenty of grass for them to eat and they grew strong and healthy.

Then the Civil War began. Most of the Texas men went away to fight and the cattle were left to run wild.

After the war ended, people in many parts of the country needed cattle for meat and other products. A Texas rancher who could gather a herd of cattle could get a good price for them. But first he had to take the cattle to market towns like Abilene and Dodge City.

The trip north was long and dangerous. A rancher needed strong young men who were good at riding horses to drive the cattle to market. So he hired a crew of cowboys. The time of the long cattle drives lasted only about fifteen years. This is the story of the cowboys during the first exciting years of the long drives.

The ranchers were the pioneers of the cattle country. Instead of farming the land, they grazed cattle. There were very few schools and churches, and the houses were as many as fifty miles apart. Few women and children lived in cattle country in the early days. Those who did led a rugged and lonely life.

A man who decided to raise and sell cattle had to find a spot with plenty of grass and water. He usually built his ranch house near a stream. The house had a kitchen, or mess hall, where all the cowboys ate their meals. Nearby was a corral where the horses were trained and a bunkhouse where the cowboys slept.

A cowboy's workday started early. The cook and the wrangler were out of the bunkhouse before sunrise. The wrangler was the youngest member of the outfit. He took care of the cowboys' horses. He also helped the cook prepare their meals. Bacon, salt pork, baked beans, and sourdough biscuits—washed down with strong coffee—were some of the things the cowboys ate.

In hot weather the cowboys ate their meals around an open fire. After supper, they usually played cards or dominoes. Some of them worked on repairing their gear. And one of the men usually played music on a fiddle, a mouth organ, or a banjo. But most of the cowboys were so tired at the end of the day that they quickly went to sleep.

Because of the hard life, cowboys often looked older than they were. When riding on the trail, they spent up to eighteen hours a day on horseback, in all kinds of weather. The special clothes a cowboy wore were very practical. A wide-brimmed felt hat shielded his face from rain and hot sun. It could also be used as a pail to scoop water from a stream, and a pillow to rest on at night.

On windy days or during a stampede, a cowboy tied a bandanna around his face to keep dust out of his nose. He also used his bandanna to blindfold a frightened horse. Heavy chaps made of leather or animal skins protected the cowboy's legs from thorns and scratchy brush. Most cowboys did not own much—not even the horses they rode. But every cowboy owned his own saddle. A saddle cost a great deal of money, but it lasted a long time.

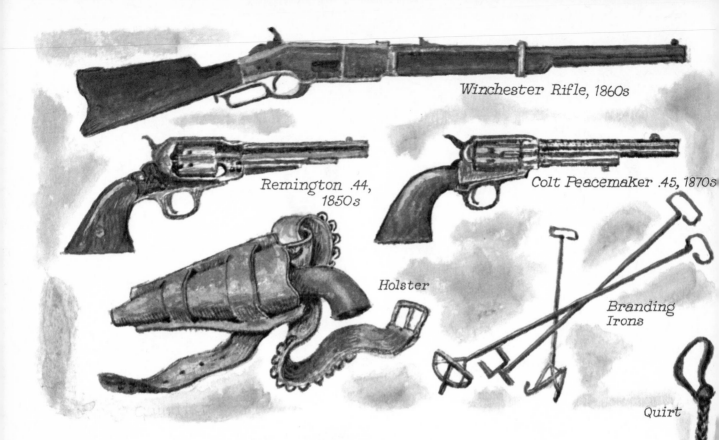

Winchester Rifle, 1860s

Remington .44, 1850s

Colt Peacemaker .45, 1870s

Holster

Branding Irons

Quirt

The cowboys almost always carried a six-shooter. Though it did not shoot very accurately, it could be used to turn back a stampede, blast away at a rattlesnake, or stop an angry cow. Rifles were useful for hunting wolves or coyotes that might attack the herd. A cowboy changed horses several times a day to keep from wearing his horses out. But he always used the same saddle. The shape of the saddle kept a rider from slipping backward when his horse stopped short or reared. Cowboy boots had high heels so the rider's feet would not slip through the stirrups. The high tops kept out dirt and pebbles, and protected the cowboy's ankles from snake bites. Spurs were used to make the horse move quickly. So was the leather quirt, or whip, which most cowboys did not like to use.

Saddle

Lasso

Bit

Plains Stetson

Bridle

Texas Hat

Boot

Spur

To catch cattle and horses, cowboys used a lasso, or lariat, made of strong hemp rope. A roper on horseback kept his lasso tied to his saddle horn. In these illustrations a cowboy on foot is roping a horse. The slipknot allows him to make the loop any size he wants. He lets out extra line to make the loop large enough to fit around the horse's head. He whirls the loop in the air to keep it open. Then he aims and tosses it over the horse's head.

Cowboys rode small, tough mustangs—often called cow ponies. Mustangs ran wild on the range, so they had to be caught and tamed. A wild horse will buck and kick if anything is put on its back. Bronco busters saddled and bridled the mustangs and cured them of bucking. Cowboys trained a different horse for each special task—night riding, swimming rivers, or working in heavy brush. Though the rancher usually owned the horses, the cowboys were very attached to them.

Roundup took place twice a year—in spring and fall. Sometimes it lasted for weeks. Since there were no fences on the open range, herds from several different ranches sometimes wandered for miles and miles. Often they mingled with each other. Each rancher had a special brand that marked his cattle as his own. At roundup time his cowboys searched all over the range, gathering his cattle together in bunches.

As soon as the cattle had been gathered, the cowboys drove them to their day's camp. This was never easy because the cows did not like to be moved from their grazing spots. At the camp, newborn calves and mavericks—strays that had not been branded before—were roped and marked with the branding irons.

After spring roundup, the drive north to market began. A drover or trail boss took charge of the herd. He kept a careful count of the cattle because several ranchers usually joined herds for the drive. The trail boss was followed by six teams of cowboys who rode around the herd, guiding and prodding the cattle along the trail.

On the first few days of the long drive, the men drove the cattle as far as they could so the animals would not try to return to the home range. The famous Chisholm Trail from Texas to Abilene, Kansas, was 1,000 miles long. Day and night, for almost three months, the cowboys worked to get the cattle to market. Crossing rivers was only one of the dangers along the way.

In Indian Territory, the Indians had the right to charge a toll.
If the trail boss did not pay, the Indians would not let the cattle go
through. Sometimes they would stampede the herd, sending the wild
and frightened animals running away from the trail. Some very small

thing could cause a stampede—lightning, a strange smell, or the lighting of a match. Prairie fires were often started by cattle thieves, who were called rustlers. While the cowboys put out the fire, the rustlers would capture as many stampeding cattle as they could.

THE OLD CHISHOLM TRAIL

Come-a-long boys and listen to my tale, S'll
tell you of my troubles on the old Chisholm trail come-a
ti yi yip pee come-a ti yi yea come-a
ti-yi- yip-pee , come-a ti-yi - yea .....

2.
Oh, a ten dollar hoss and a forty dollar saddle
and I'm goin' to punchin' Texas cattle.... etc.

3.
It's cloudy in the west a-lookin' like rain,
And my durned ol' slicker's in the wagon again.
....etc.

At sundown the cattle were sent off the trail to graze. Then they settled down for the night. Every cowboy took a turn on watch. Two or three cowboys usually worked together, circling the herd for about two hours. The cowboys often sang songs to quiet the herd and make the night watch less lonesome. Once the herd was quiet, the cook prepared the outfit's night meal. The chuckwagon held all the food, cooking utensils, and extra supplies for the drive.

The Chisholm Trail ended at the cowtown of Abilene. From there the railroad took the cattle to cities in the East. By this time most of the cowboys were eager to get into town. But they had to hold the cattle a few miles outside of Abilene until the stockyards were clear of other herds. Cattle buyers from the East often came out to look the cattle over.

In the early days of the Chisholm Trail, the cowboys who drove the cattle to market also loaded them onto the trains. The cattle did not like to be forced into the stuffy boxcars. The men had to use long, pointed poles to hurry the mooing, angry cattle along. That is how cowboys came to be called *cowpokes* or *cowpunchers*.

In just five years, more than a million head of cattle came up the Chisholm Trail to Abilene. Soon the town began to receive more cattle than it could handle. The people who lived there did not like the cowboys. When the railroad was extended farther west to Dodge City, the center of the cattle trade moved west too.

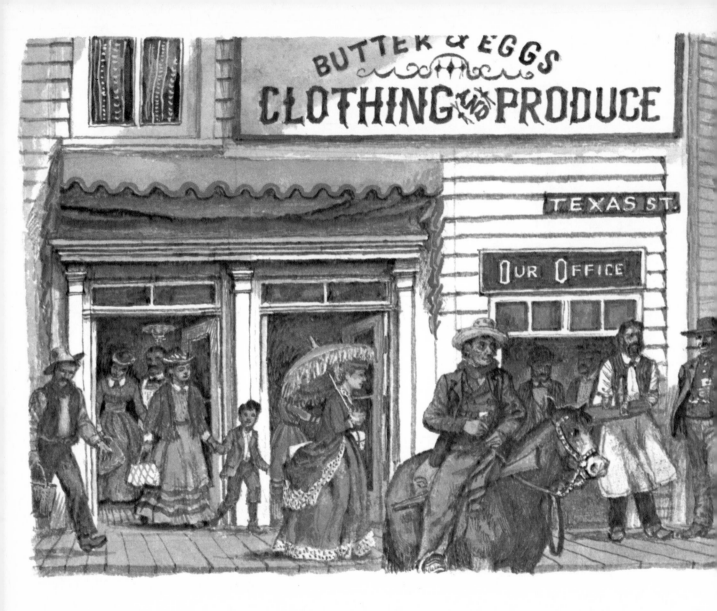

By the time all the work was done, the cowboys were ready for fun. But after three months on the trail, they were dirty and badly in need of a shave and a haircut. Their clothes were torn and worn out. With their pay in hand, the cowboys went to a rooming house for a bath. Then they bought new clothes and visited the barber.

Though the cowboys were not allowed to carry their six-shooters in town, they often became rowdy, drinking too much whiskey and starting fights. The townspeople tried to put an end to their drunkenness and misbehavior. After a while, they had to hire town marshals to keep peace.

Charles Goodnight

Mary Ann Goodnight

Jesse Chisholm

Joseph G. McCoy

Texas Ranger

Many people became famous during the days of the cowboys. Charles Goodnight, who had once been a cowboy himself, owned one of the largest cattle ranches in Texas. His wife, Mary Ann, was the only woman for hundreds of miles around his huge ranch. The Chisholm Trail was named after Jesse Chisholm, a well-known guide and trader. Joseph G. McCoy set up the town of Abilene. The Texas Rangers introduced the cowboys to the six-shooter.

Calamity Jane  Buffalo Bill Cody  Billy the Kid  Cole Younger  Jesse James  Belle Starr

After fighting in the Texas war for independence, the Texas Rangers became law enforcers in the West. Calamity Jane (Jane Canary) was a tobacco-chewing, sharp-shooting pal to many cowboys. Buffalo Bill Cody started his career as a pony express rider. Later he put together his touring *Wild West Show*. Billy the Kid, Cole Younger, Jesse James, and Belle Starr were all notorious outlaws.

The cowboys who did not stay to work in Abilene usually took the train east to the Mississippi River. From there they traveled south by steamboat. They might have spent all their money, but they still had their saddles and their gear.

As soon as they were back in Texas, the cowboys usually signed up with a rancher to ride the trail again.